ALIEN IN MY POCKET

Space Invaders

ALIEN IN MY POCKET

Space Invaders

by
Nate Ball

illustrated by
Macky Pamintuan

HARPER
An Imprint of HarperCollins*Publishers*

Alien in My Pocket: Space Invaders

Text by Nate Ball, copyright © 2016 by HarperCollins Publishers

Illustrations by Macky Pamintuan, copyright © 2016 by HarperCollins Publishers

All rights reserved. Printed in the United States of America.

No part of this book may be used or reproduced in any manner whatsoever without written permission except in the case of brief quotations embodied in critical articles and reviews. For information address HarperCollins Children's Books, a division of HarperCollins Publishers, 195 Broadway, New York, NY 10007.

Library of Congress Control Number: 2015933468

ISBN 978-0-06-237092-1 (trade bdg.)—ISBN 978-0-06-237091-4 (pbk.)

Typography by Jeff Shake

16 17 18 19 20   PC/RRDH   10 9 8 7 6 5 4 3 2 1

❖

First Edition

Contents

The Mess I Made

It's hard to be a kid these days.

Think about it.

You've got chores, tons of homework, and little brothers. Moms and dads are always bossing you around and saying they know best. Coaches make sour faces every time you take batting practice. And teachers think learning is the most exciting thing ever invented.

It can all be a bit much for a fourth grader to handle without going nuts.

Now add to all that the responsibility of ensuring the survival of the human race, and you get a glimpse into my life.

I've pretty much gone nutty.

And it's easy to pinpoint exactly when it all went wrong: the day Amp arrived.

Amp is the avocado-size alien who burst into my life when he flew through my window screen. His football-size spaceship dented my bedroom wall and crash-landed on my bed.

Connecting the dots from that first, shocking night to the possible end of mankind wasn't easy to do. But that didn't mean it was any less true. Because that moment so many months ago really had led directly to this night. Earth—and the billions of people living on it—was in serious crisis, even if they didn't know it yet.

Which was, more or less, what I was thinking about as I flew through the cool night in my underwear. I was clinging to Amp's spaceship for dear life as an army of soldiers chased me from below and an alien force poised to invade Earth floated above me in the starry sky.

As I said, it was an odd time for a kid whose biggest accomplishment previously had been making the travel baseball team as a catcher with a pretty decent throw to second base and a so-so batting average.

Despite all that, the world was counting on me. Now if I could only find some pants.

3

Face-Plant

Amp landed near Olivia and her grandfather.

Or I should say, Amp dumped me off the top of his spaceship from about eight feet in the air, and I face-planted onto some sharp pine needles near Olivia and her grandfather. Then Amp landed safely, all comfy cozy inside his spaceship.

Olivia and her grandfather had been waiting for us to return to make our getaway, which I now realized would be harder than we'd expected. The dark woods around us were filled with the sound of men shouting orders. Beams of light flashed through the trees. An army helicopter with a superbright searchlight roared above us.

The soldiers in the fort from which we had just escaped were coming after us. They were determined not to let us get away easily.

5

Olivia emerged out of the darkness to help me up. "Why . . . why are you wearing only your unmentionables? Wh-where are your pants?" she stammered. "And your shoes and socks and shirt?"

"Kind of hard to explain," I said, gasping and plucking off dried pine needles. I stumbled, trying to shake the dizziness. The woods spun around me. I put my hands on my knees and concentrated on not throwing up.

Olivia ran to the truck. Her grandfather was on one knee by Amp's ship. It steamed visibly and had a slight golden glow to it. It looked more futuristic out here in the woods than it had under the wool blanket in my closet, which was where it had sat, unused, for weeks.

"We've got to get out of here," Olivia said, handing me her grandfather's vest.

I zipped it up, but it was way too big. I felt like I was wearing a dress.

"Step into these," Olivia demanded, setting down huge, waterproof hunting boots.

I did as she said, and my toes searched the inside of the giant boots for warmth. I glanced down at myself and held my arms out. "I look ridiculous!"

She gave a small, nervous laugh. "You look cute." She punched me on the arm.

"Oh, brother," I said.

"They're coming," Olivia's grandfather noted, climbing into the cab of his truck through the passenger side. He had Amp's spaceship under his arm. "Let's go, you two."

Seconds later we were driving along the twisting road that ran through the woods. The helicopters were still buzzing around in the sky, so we had to drive with the headlights off. Nobody spoke. My fingers gripped the dashboard so hard, they ached.

"Is he really in there?" Olivia's grandfather said, stealing a glance down at the spaceship that now sat in Olivia's lap. "Your friend? Is he really inside that thing?"

"Yes, Grandpa," Olivia said. "You'll like him. He's weird, but he's totally harmless."

"He's normally not so shy," I said. "Honestly, he never stops jabbering. You want to meet him?"

"Not right now. Let's keep him in there, okay?" he said quietly.

"Oh, Amp kind of does what he wants when he wants," Olivia explained. "In fact, he usually does exactly what you don't want him to do." She cleared her throat. "Sorry, Grandpa, for keeping Amp a secret. Zack and I decided not to tell anyone."

"We thought that would be best for everybody," I put in.

He grunted, his face pushed out over the steering wheel to better concentrate on the road.

Then Olivia's grandfather braked suddenly and peered at the woods on the right side.

"Did you see something?" I asked with alarm. "What is it?"

"A bear?" Olivia said. "A deer? Army guys? Aliens? Bigfoot?"

He shushed us and slowed the truck even more. He flipped on the parking lights, which lit the road in front of us with a dim yellow glow. I was glad to have even a little bit of light to guide us, but now we were barely moving.

"Are we running out of gas?" Olivia asked. "That would not be good timing."

"Do you have to go to the bathroom?" I asked, searching his face, which was now lit by the weak light coming from the dashboard. I could see his face was creased with focus.

I kept turning around to look down the road behind us, expecting to see army truck headlights roaring.

"Yeah, a potty break right now would be pretty lame, Grandpa," Olivia said. She turned to me.

"Sometimes people Grandpa's age can't help—"

"Shush, you two," he said. We were now going about only five miles per hour. "They'll set up roadblocks at the end of this valley."

We thought about that for a moment.

"That is so intense," Olivia said quietly.

"There it is," Olivia's grandfather said with relief in his voice.

We turned slowly off the smooth main road and onto a bumpy gravel path. The truck squeaked and groaned in protest.

A dim, single lightbulb appeared out of the darkness above a cracked and faded sign that said BENNETT LAKE PARK.

I checked behind us one last time as we left the road; nobody was in hot pursuit. Yet.

"Came to fish here a few times," Olivia's grandfather said, and sighed. "Terrible fishing. Trout no bigger than your hand."

After a minute a locked gate appeared in front of us next to a deserted ranger station hut where people must have to pay to enter the park during fishing season. The truck turned and rolled slowly into the small dirt parking space next to the hut.

We parked with most of the truck pushed into the bushes. I could hear a few twigs snap as the truck moved forward. The branches of a giant tree slapped at the top of the truck's cab and hung low over its bed. It was a good hiding place.

"Wait, is this a potty break?" Olivia asked.

"Nope," Olivia's grandfather said, turning the key and plunging us into silence.

We sat in the dark. The engine clicked and gurgled as it cooled down. I heard an owl hoot nearby.

"We are going to break into that ranger station and use it to figure out a plan."

"Isn't that illegal?" I asked.

"Oh, I imagine we've already broken a few dozen federal and state laws tonight," he said with a hint of humor in his voice.

I rubbed my chilled arms. "Do you think we're on the FBI's ten most wanted list?" I asked.

"No"—Olivia's grandfather sighed—"but the night is still young."

"You can meet Amp when we get inside," Olivia said excitedly. "He's never really met an adult before. He is so funny."

"We also might want to discuss preventing the destruction of Earth and everyone who lives on it," I mumbled.

"That might be good," Olivia's grandfather said, opening his door.

"Yes, we can do that after some introductions," Olivia said.

"The next hour or so may determine the fate of human race," I said quietly.

"Oh, don't be so dramatic, Wacky Zacky," Olivia said, smacking me on my bare knee. "You'll scare Grandpa."

"Oh, don't worry," he said. "I'm scared enough already."

"That makes two of us," I said.

Mr. Larry

"You look like an elf!" Amp exclaimed when he finally poked his head out of his still-glowing ship. Apparently, he found my outfit humorous. He laughed and slapped one of his three-fingered hands on the side of his spaceship. "Zack, you've just got to take a selfie. That is too good not to share."

"Oh, shut up," I said, looking down at my bony legs, which felt like two pieces of uncooked spaghetti.

"Amp, this is my grandfather," Olivia said. "His name is Larry."

"Larry?" I whispered. "I never knew that."

Olivia's grandfather nodded silently, his eyes big circles of disbelief. His mouth hung open a bit in shock. He was backed into the dark corner of the tiny guard hut.

We had discovered the hut had no electricity, so now a small flashlight from the truck lit up the inside of the squeezed-in space. Strange shadows bounced off the walls. There wasn't even room to sit down.

"He looks like he's seen a ghost," Amp said cheerfully in his high-pitched voice.

"Oh, you're a lot creepier than a ghost," I said. "Trust me."

"He's never met an alien before?" Amp asked Olivia quietly.

"You're everybody's first alien," I said.

"Ampy, you forget how weird-looking you are," Olivia said, patting her grandfather's arm. "He takes about three months to get used to, Grandpa."

"I'm still not used to him," I mumbled.

Amp jumped down onto the bare wooden board that served as a sort of shelf-and-table combo. "I am Amp, Scout First Class from the planet Erde. At your service. Pleasure to meet you, Mr. Larry." Amp bowed dramatically and made a little circular wave with his hand.

Mr. Larry just nodded, still staring. He covered his open mouth with his hand. It would take some time.

"Where are we?" Amp asked. "It smells like bear farts in here. Is anyone standing on a dead raccoon?" He grabbed his neck and stumbled about. "Can we a least crack open the door and let some fresh air in here?"

"Please don't act like this," I hissed. "You're freaking out Mr. Larry."

"The door is locked from the outside with a big fat chain and lock," Olivia explained.

"We all had to climb through there," I said, pointing at the window where a park ranger probably took people's money.

"Grandpa popped it open with a screwdriver," Olivia said.

"It is kind of cozy," Amp said, looking around. "Except for the smell of whale puke in here." He laughed and looked at each of us. He was the only one laughing.

"This is serious," Olivia said tightly.

"Yeah, your Erdian friends are already here," I said.

Olivia pointed up. "They're floating in the sky. Right now. Waiting."

"Oh, right," Amp said. "We better . . ."

He didn't finish. The humor faded from his face.

"They're about to attack at any minute, aren't they?" I asked.

"Oh dear," he said, as if the seriousness of the situation were occurring to him for the first time.

04

Space and Swiss Cheese

"Something's not right," Amp said, stroking his tiny chin.

"Something?" I croaked. "You mean everything! We just kidnapped the world's first alien after breaking into a government facility. There's an army of soldiers who've blocked the roads and sent up a half dozen helicopters to find us. And there's an Erdian army floating in the sky about to attack Earth. That's no 'something'—that's everything."

Amp stared at me for a second. "Point taken."

"We are in way over our heads here, guys," I said.

"Honestly, none of this makes sense," Amp said,

chewing on his lip. "Why haven't they attacked? Why are they holding formation? That's not how Erdians do things. What are they doing up there?"

"Maybe they changed their minds," Olivia said with shrug.

"You don't risk traveling with a million Erdians through space and time, then change your mind once you get here," Amp said, waving his arms in frustration.

"I'm sure they don't want to hurt you, Ampy," Olivia put in hopefully. "They know you're down here and don't want to zap you by accident or blow you up or vaporize you . . . or whatever."

"That wouldn't worry them." Amp sighed, shaking his head.

"Vaporize?" I croaked. "That sounds painful."

"Oh, it shouldn't be painful," Amp said. "It's actually over very quick." He snapped his blue fingers.

Olivia and I looked at each other.

Olivia's grandfather shuffled his feet. His arms were folded tight, his eyes scrunched up as he studied Amp like he was a simple card trick that could be figured out if you watched it carefully enough.

We had heard a few helicopters buzz over in the last few minutes, looking for us, but they obviously hadn't seen the truck because it was parked so far under the big tree outside.

"Hey!" I said, suddenly pounding my fist on the shelf Amp stood on. I had only meant to get his attention, but my thump on the flimsy wood buckled it and sent Amp pinwheeling into the air. The flashlight flickered and fell over with a thwack and rolled away. Amp summersaulted in the air and landed on his butt.

Olivia grabbed the flashlight before it could roll off the shelf. She stood the flashlight back up so its light beam lit the little hut again.

I sucked air in between my clenched teeth. "Oh my gosh, sorry about that!"

"You scared the brimbles out of me!" Amp yelled.

"Brimbles?" Olivia giggled. "That's a new one."

"I was just trying to make a point," I exclaimed. "I didn't mean to knock the pimples off you."

"Use your words, not your fists!" Amp shouted. "And it's brimbles, not pimples. Erdians don't get skin blemishes."

I took a deep breath. "Whatever. I said sorry. My point was that there's a lot you don't under-stand, Amp. It was only a few hours ago that you thought your planet had exploded and you were the last Erdian left in the universe. Let's be hon-est: Half the time you don't know what's going on. That's not news."

"Harsh," Olivia said. "But kinda true, little man."

"Don't call me little man!" Amp said, jump-ing back to his feet. He started pacing around in circles, the way he always did when he was thinking hard.

"You haven't even explained how you can travel through space and time," Olivia said.

Amp stopped and held up a single finger. His eyes got big.

I slapped my forehead. "Please, Olivia, not another teachable moment."

Amp straightened his back and got into his teaching pose. "Oh, time travel is actually quite simple, children, yet incredibly complicated at the same time."

"Oh, thanks for clearing that up for us, Professor No Pants," I said, rolling my eyes.

Amp flicked his antennas, enjoying the chance to show off. "Let me simplify it for you: Think of time as a giant slice of Swiss cheese, a slice so wide that you can never reach the edge of it."

"Now you're just making me hungry," I mumbled.

"Time sounds delicious," Olivia said.

Amp tried to shush us with his hands. "Now, we are located at a fixed point on that slice of Swiss cheese, meaning stuck at a certain point in time. Get it?"

"Like a nut in the cheese," I said.

"Swiss cheese doesn't have nuts," Olivia corrected.

"I know, I was just—"

"Would you two just listen?" Amp exploded. "I'm trying to teach you something."

"Lessons at the end of the world." I sighed.

"We are fixed at a point on that slice of Swiss cheese," he repeated, "as we are fixed at a certain point in time. Is that clear?"

"It's pretty clear I could go for a ham-and-cheese sandwich right now," I said.

Amp growled at me. "But that slice of Swiss cheese is really a block of Swiss cheese, a block of cheese as thick as the universe."

"That is a lot of cheese," Olivia whispered.

I shook my head. "Wait. What?" I said. "My skull just filled with brain soup!"

Amp grunted. "Time is just one dimension of the cheese, the length of the slice," he said, slapping his hands together, which I guess represented the cheese. "But," he said dramatically, moving his hands as far away from each other as he could, "this cheese is not sliced thin—it's very, very, very

27

thick. Thicker than your mind can even imagine."

"I'm lost," I said. "And you're making my stomach growl."

"Are you saying you travel through the holes in that Swiss cheese?" Olivia's grandfather said suddenly.

We all turned in surprise.

"That is perfectly correct, Mr. Gary!" Amp exclaimed.

"It's Mr. Larry, Amp," Olivia corrected, poking Amp in the stomach with a finger.

"Like a wormhole," Mr. Larry said quietly, "through space and time."

"Finally, a man of science and learning!" Amp exclaimed, clapping. "Very good, Mr. Harry."

"Oh my gosh, it's Mr. *Larry*!" Olivia corrected again. "C'mon, it's not a hard name!"

"Isn't that what I said?" Amp said, looking around, confused.

I sighed. "Guys, we've got bigger fish to fry," I said.

"What is it with you and your stomach?" Amp said. "We do not have time to catch and prepare fish right now."

Olivia put her face in front of Amp. "No, that's just an expression. 'We have bigger fish to fry' means we have more important things to do than to discuss Swiss cheese. Now, let's—"

Suddenly we all froze as the thunder of a low-flying helicopter filled the air, its whooping blades vibrating everything around us. We could see its powerful beam of light explode through tiny cracks in the roof of the ranger hut. The entire wooden structure seemed to shiver in fear. Dust filled the air. The helicopter did not fly on. Its engine roared above us again. It was circling!

"Oh dear!" Amp shouted, staring up at the ceiling.

"They've found us!" Olivia's grandpa shouted above the noise. "We've got to go before we're surrounded."

"GO WHERE?!" Olivia and I screamed.

"Follow me!" he commanded, and started climbing out the window, Amp's ship tucked under his arm.

"A man of action! Lead the way, Mr.—" Amp began, but I snatched him up before he could finish, and stuffed him into a giant pocket of my man-size vest. I zipped the pocket before he could poke his head out.

We had talked enough.

Now it was time for action . . . before we ran out of Swiss cheese.

05

End of the Line

I had lost a boot.

And it wasn't even mine!

It was now somewhere back in the woods, sucked off my foot as I ran through a patch of squishy mud.

The soldiers behind me had probably already plucked it out.

Now I ran lopsided through the woods, trying to keep up with Olivia and her grandfather.

The vest I was wearing didn't provide much protection. My bare arms and legs where getting lashed by branches, twigs, and rough tree bark. Even worse, my bare foot felt like it had been jabbed with a thousand darts.

Add on top of all this the fact that I was colder than a Popsicle, and you get an idea of how our escape was going.

The trees around us were providing cover from the helicopters above, but the dozen or so soldiers following me had arrived incredibly quickly. And they wore boots that fit. They weren't far behind us, and they were clearly gaining ground fast. I could hear the distant snap of twigs behind me and see the occasional flash of a far-off flashlight.

My big gasps of breath were instantly turned into puffy clouds.

"Boy, you are out of shape," Amp said inside my head.

I had almost forgotten about the passenger in my pocket. "Oh, shut up," I replied without speaking.

I'd learned pretty quickly after he'd crash-landed in my room that Amp could communicate with his mind, and I could communicate back. But there was something odd about having that little voice inside my head coming from somebody else. It was uncomfortable, not unlike wearing another man's boots.

I burst through some scratchy bushes and almost fell into Bennett Lake.

I crouched at the edge of the water as tiny, freezing waves lapped at my bare foot. A full moon hung low over the trees on the opposite side of the lake and lit the water like a giant mirror.

"Hey, why did we stop?!" Amp shouted in my head. "GO, GO, GO!"

"Please, stay outta my head," I replied with my mind, looking over my shoulder for any sign of the soldiers in hot pursuit.

"Are you surrounded? Did you break your leg? I've been hearing a lot of things snapping out there. What do you see? Can you unzip this pocket, please?"

"Zip it, Amp. I can't hear myself think." I gasped out loud.

"Zip it? No, I said unzip it! I can't see anything. And it's so stuffy in here."

"Would you shush up?" I looked to the right and couldn't see anybody.

"Do you have a cramp? Quick—hold your arms above your head!"

I looked left and could see Olivia about fifty yards away, running on the edge of the water. I followed clumsily along the pebbly shore, my foot happy at least to be out of the splintery forest.

It looked like Olivia and her grandfather were heading for an empty wooden dock. I could see Olivia's grandfather running down it in the moonlight.

That seemed like a spectacularly bad idea to me. If they found us, we'd be trapped!

"No!" I tried to shout, but I was breathing too hard to be heard. Plus, I didn't want to give away our location to the troops on our tail.

"STOP! DO NOT TAKE ANOTHER STEP!" a man's voice ordered from behind me. "THEY'RE OVER HERE! BY THE LAKE!" he hollered to the other soldiers.

I could hear him splashing his boots along the shore as he came after me. The woods to my left exploded with voices. I could see flashlights through the trees. This was impossible!

Olivia and her grandfather were almost to the end of the dock by the time I had just hit its first rough boards.

I instantly got a nasty splinter in my heel. "Brimples!" I yelped in pain and frustration, but I kept going. What other choice did I have?

I looked back and was nearly blinded by flash-light beams. We were indeed backed into a corner. The first of the National Guard soldiers to arrive had bunched down where the dock began. They were preparing for their final assault.

When I turned back around, Olivia and her grandfather were gone.

Gone?

"Wha . . . ?" I gasped.

35

Were we swimming across this giant lake?! I was a terrible swimmer. And it was freezing. We would all drown. We would all die. This was a terrible idea. I stopped, squeezed both sides of my head, and blew clouds of my breath into the chilly air.

GONE?

I was somehow alone. My mind spun.

I turned and faced the soldiers as they started down the dock toward me.

"We are at the end of the line, my friend," I said loud enough for Amp to hear me.

Showdown

But then, out the corner of my eye, I saw a large shape moving in the water.

"Zack, jump!" Olivia's voice came out of the dark.

She was slowly moving away from the dock in a tiny rowboat. Her grandfather was next to her, looking back over his shoulder as he steered a tiny outboard engine that made no noise.

I hesitated.

I froze just long enough that I knew I would never make the boat if I jumped, even with a running start. The boat was already silently sliding out into the inky black water.

"ZACK!" Olivia screamed.

I took a step toward the boat but stopped myself. I'd never make it. And honestly, I was

more of a sinker than a swimmer.

I shot a look at the approaching soldiers who were now inching forward, each with their hands raised in a don't-panic-kid-everything-will-be-just-fine gesture.

I knew what I had to do.

I unzipped the side pocket on my vest and pulled out Amp.

"Holy hot dogs! It's about time!" he screeched in his squeaky voice, sucking in air in his overly dramatic style.

The soldiers in front of me gasped. Many had not seen Amp firsthand, and the shock of seeing him stopped them in their tracks.

Of course Amp barely even noticed them. He was too busy complaining to me: "Are you trying to kill me? Now I have a crick in my neck. And I've got a headache! I may be an alien, but I need air as much as—" He stopped when he noticed the crowd of a dozen soldiers huffing and puffing just ten feet away. "Oh dear," he said quietly.

"Swim!" Olivia yelled desperately from the dark. The shape of the small white boat was already fading into the misty darkness. "Swim for it, Zack!"

I shook my head. I had a better idea.

"DON'T MOVE!" I screamed at the soldiers, raising Amp in my fist and shaking him around in the air above my head. "Or I will squeeze this alien until he pops like a water balloon!"

"How rude!" Amp screeched, wriggling around in my fist.

"C'mon, kid, give us all a break and hand the creature over," the soldier who was out front growled. "We need to bring it back alive."

"Creature? Really?" Amp shrieked angrily. "How dare you. I am from an advanced civilization, sir!"

I decided to speak with my mind so the soldiers wouldn't know what I was up to. "Amp," I said with my brain, "act like I'm squeezing you to death."

"That won't be hard," he said, gasping.

I took a step toward the solders and shook Amp in my fist. "I'll do it!" I threatened. "Back up! All of you! Or I'll squeeze the life out of this alien!"

"I can't breath!" Amp screamed as if on cue. "Hey, you soldiers! This kid is crazy! Look in his eyes. He's nutso. I don't want to pop and squirt all over this dock like a jelly doughnut! Please back up before my eyes explode out of my face! I think one of my toes just fell off!"

Amp was enjoying himself a little too much. I think he loved playing the role of a hostage.

"My brains might start leaking out of my antennas!"

"Okay, okay, take it easy," I said with my mind. "Jeepers."

My idea had worked well enough. The soldiers had moved back a good ten feet. Plenty of room for what I needed to do next.

"Hey, it's working," Amp said inside my head. "Brilliant. But now what?"

Without answering, I spun back around toward the lake, took two quick skips and one giant leap, and threw Amp as hard as I could.

"NOOOOOOOOOOOOOOOOOOOOoooooo ooooo!" Amp's scream faded as he disappeared into the mist that hung above the lake.

As soon as I threw him, I instinctively knew he'd land in the boat.

It was the same feeling I got when I threw a baseball to pick off a player trying to steal second base on me.

A good catcher knows as soon as the baseball leaves his hand if he's put enough heat on it. My coach loved my throws to second. He said they were the best he'd ever seen from someone my age. And with the throw I'd just made, the runner would be out by a mile—so Amp would be just fine.

I let out the breath I had been holding in and

turned slowly around to face the very unhappy soldiers who were now glaring at me like I had just sat on their birthday cakes.

"Does anyone have tweezers?" I said simply. "I've got a splinter that's killing me."

"You should not have thrown the creature, kid," the lead soldier said in a spooky voice, his hands closing into angry fists.

43

Punch It

"**W**hy did you throw the alien, kid?"

"Do you know how much trouble you're in?"

"Who sent you? Who do you work for?"

"Where the heck are your pants?"

"Can that alien even swim?"

"Where did you hide the spaceship?"

"Who are those two people in the boat?"

"Why are you wearing only one boot?"

The questions from the soldiers surrounding me came fast and furious. Too fast for me to really answer any of them. They all seemed upset that I hadn't followed their orders.

I hadn't really planned what I'd do after I threw Amp onto the boat. Now I was worried they'd toss me into the lake out of sheer frustration.

I looked around at all of them. "What alien?" I
said with a fake smile.

This wasn't what they wanted to hear. The soldiers seemed to tense up as a group.

"What do we do, Sarge?" one of the soldiers

asked the man out front, who appeared to be the leader.

Sarge just shook his head and squinted at me. "Maybe this kid's on the side of the enemy. Maybe he's a traitor. Maybe he's friends with the invader."

"Who? Amp? Oh, he's my friend all right," I said. "He's my best friend, in fact." My teeth started to clack together as my whole body began to shiver from the cold.

That was when somebody—out of nowhere— punched me right in the stomach.

I buckled and flew out over the edge of the dock. I was sure I was going into the water— whether I wanted to or not.

With my eyes squeezed shut, I waited for the shock of the ice-cold water.

But it never came.

Man, I must have been punched hard because I was still flying backward.

Something wasn't right.

That was when I realized I hadn't been hit in the stomach by a fist—it was Amp's spaceship! I was clutching it as it pressed into my guts.

"Hold on tight," Amp said inside my head.

For the third time that night, I was taken on a wobbly air-bound trip on Amp's ship.

The flat, moonlit water skimmed past below me, just inches from my feet. I noticed the millions of stars reflected on the surface of the lake. I wondered how deep the water was. I thought of sharks. My mind must have drifted because my foot with the heavy boot on it hit the water and was pulled off.

The impact of the boot snagging on the water sent the spaceship spinning. My body helicoptered over the lake.

I hated flying this way.

I was too scared to throw up. I groaned in the dark.

And then, without warning, I was deposited into the boat, which had appeared out of the darkness. The back of my head must have hit Olivia's knee because I cried out in pain, and so did she.

I was dizzy. The world spun around me. But I was safe.

"Look what the catfish dragged in," Olivia's grandfather said calmly. "Welcome back, Zack."

"You almost broke my kneecap," Olivia said, wheezing.

"Hey, I wasn't driving," I said, and gasped. The stars in the sky swirled above me as my brain tried to stop turning inside my skull.

"Sorry, Mr. Larry, but I lost both of your boots," I said as I sat on one of the wooden planks that served as the boat's seats.

"At least we're safe from those goons," Olivia's grandfather said.

Amp's spaceship lowered onto the one open plank of wood. The door of the spaceship clicked open, and Amp popped his head out.

"Gosh, Amp, were you purposely trying to make me seasick?" I said. "If I wasn't so hungry, I would have puked all over the lake."

"Flying is easy; levitating not so much," Amp said.

"What's the difference?" Olivia asked. "Isn't levitating magic?"

"Oh no," I groaned. "It's another teachable moment."

"Let's talk about hovering and levitation," Amp said. "It's quite fascinating."

"Do we have to?" I mumbled.

Amp began speaking into the tiny wrist recorder he wore:

"Note to Erdian Council . . ."

"I told you this would happen," I said, shaking my head at Olivia.

"Children are fascinated by the concept of hovering, as our spaceships appear to do. They seem unaware, however, of the science behind hovering and levitation. Of course, both involve providing enough upward force to counteract the downward force of gravity. Hovering in a stationary position requires mechanical means and considerable energy, as seen on this planet with hummingbirds, bees, dragonflies, and helicopters."

"Oh, I love how hummingbirds can just hang

out in the air in front of a flower," Olivia said.

Amp didn't acknowledge Olivia's comment. He was on a roll.

"Must explain that levitation is different because it provides sufficient upward force without mechanical means, for example through electrostatic or aerodynamic means—or, as in the case of the *Dingle*, through magnetic fields. And while generating sufficient magnetic force to resist the effects of gravity is complex, the stability of this system took us several hundred years to figure out and perfect. Perhaps a lesson in Erdian scientific history is needed."

"Oh, please, not now," I said, groaning. "The world is still spinning around me."

Several bright, white dots appeared on the side of Amp's ship.

I sat up. "What do those white lights mean, Amp?"

"Oh . . . ," he said, his arm slowly dropping. His face grew grim with concern. "That means they're coming."

"Who's coming?" Olivia asked in an unsteady voice, scanning the lake around us. "The soldiers? Those secret agents? Who?"

That was when I noticed the stars in the sky weren't swirling because I was dizzy; the stars themselves were moving. The thousands of stars I was looking at were actually Erdian spaceships. They were all swirling in perfect formation, like a tornado of bright little dots.

They were coming. It had started. Everything we had worked for hadn't worked at all. This was it.

My stomach clenched up even tighter.

The Erdian invasion was upon us. Literally.

And So It Began

The Erdians finally got down to business after we had drifted far out into the middle of the lake in our little rowboat.

The weak, battery-powered motor had died long ago. There were no oars on board, either. We were literally sitting ducks.

The lake was surrounded by a looming wall of black trees, which gave me a trapped feeling. It was a stadium of doom. I didn't even know which direction the dock was anymore. I had a terrible feeling of being cut off from the rest of the world, and I secretly wished all those soldiers were here right now.

The night air around us began to buzz and hum. The four of us stared up as tens of thousands of Erdian spaceships descended onto the lake. They swirled around and above our heads, and I had the distinct feeling of being inside a flushing toilet bowl.

"It's so different from this angle!" Amp shouted, climbing out of his ship.

Each of us gripped the side of the boat as it began to rock and slowly turn in a circle; the Erdian fleet was creating its own wind. The humming noise had grown quite loud. The surface of the lake sparkled as it reflected the golden glow of the swarm of ships.

My heart pounded away in my chest. I had to admit that the sight was beautiful—it was ten times better than the biggest fireworks display ever—and I had the best seat in the house.

The spinning, glowing cloud of ten thousand spaceships dropped lower and lower over the surface of the lake in perfect formation. It occurred to me that nobody in history had even seen such a thing.

With shocking precision, all the ships stopped in an instant, creating a ceiling of spaceships about ten feet over the water. In the silence that followed, I was certain I could hear my own heart beating.

A green line that looked like a backward S appeared on the side of Amp's spaceship.

"Now what?" I whispered.

"Oh no," he said, leaning so close to the glowing letter that his face turned from blue to green. "It can't be!"

"Are we about to be vaporized?" Olivia asked in a trembly voice.

"We tried our best, guys," I said, looking down. "Thanks for everything."

Mr. Larry patted me softly on the back. "I never got to see Paris." He sighed. I looked over my shoulder, and he was staring up with watery eyes at the glowing ships.

"Well?" Olivia said after a few seconds went by. "Are they about to start shooting lasers or something, Amp?"

"It's worse than that," Amp said, still staring at the glowing shape.

"What could be worse than being melted by an alien space laser?!" Olivia shouted, her voice having a hollow, inside-a-big-room quality.

"Yeah, Amp, if I get vaporized, I will never forgive you," I said.

"The Kaloofa is here," he whispered. "This has never happened."

"What the heck is a Kaloofa?" Olivia asked.

I gulped. "Is that some kind of nasty, planet-destroying weapon?"

Amp pulled his face away from the glowing backward S and looked at me, then at Olivia. "It's not a thing. It's a who."

When he didn't add anything else, Olivia grunted. "Yeah, okay, then who is that and why should we care?"

I shook my head at Amp. "Even at the end of the world you're annoying."

Amp pulled on both of his antennas and stared into the lake with an odd expression. "This 'who' only happens to be the Most Supreme Erdian Empress."

"Oh? She's come to watch the destruction, eh?" I asked.

He twisted his antennas. "My great-uncle saw her in a parade once. She even looked in his direction."

"Hey," Olivia said, "what kind of queen travels through space and time just to pick on a few kids and an old man in a boat?" She paused. "Sorry, Grandpa."

Mr. Larry made a forgiving humming sound behind me.

Amp shook his head. "No, you two don't understand. The Erdian Kaloofa is like a king, a queen, a president, Santa Claus, and the Tooth Fairy all rolled into one Erdian."

"We should have gotten her a gift," Olivia grumbled.

"This is not good," Amp said in a panicky voice. He began to pace in circles on his seat in the middle of the boat. "Look at me! I am not prepared! We need flowers. And a feast. And a band. And festive lights. And I need to take a bath. Does anyone have a toothbrush?"

"Are you joking?" Olivia snapped.

"I can throw you in the lake to clean you up," I said, angry that he would care about having a party when my planet was about to be taken over.

"It's too late," he cried. "Here she comes!"

09

The Big Kaloofa

I spotted the Kaloofa's large spaceship when the smaller, football-shaped spaceships right above us parted to let it through.

I looked across from me at Olivia, but she didn't look my way. She was having her Kaloofa moment.

The Kaloofa's spaceship was shaped like a giant, flipped-over frying pan with a shark fin glued to the top. It wasn't anything like Amp's ship or the thousands of others floating above us. Apparently, the queen rode in style.

It lowered until the handle of the frying pan gently settled on the rim of the boat, hovering— or levitating—just a few feet over the water.

I scooted to the other side of my wooden plank. Olivia, who sat near the pointy end of the little boat, looked like she was in a trance.

I wasn't sure what Mr. Larry was doing. He was sitting on the wooden plank behind me, near the back of the boat. He was probably in shock. I felt bad for getting him mixed up in this, but it was too late now.

That was when I noticed Amp lying on this back next to his spaceship, all stiff and staring up at the other Erdian ships.

"Amp! Amp!" I yelped. "Get up! Did you faint? Are you cramping up?"

"Quiet, Earthling," he whispered back between clenched teeth.

"Oh, it's 'Earthling' now?" I growled, offended. "Are you seasick or something? Stand up—your Loofa is here."

"It's the Kaloofa," he said, groaning in embarrassment.

"Snap to it," I urged him. "You look like you fell off the roof."

"This is the traditional way to greet Erdian royalty."

"That's the weirdest tradition I ever heard of."

"Says you," he snapped. "I suggest you do the same."

"There's not enough room for all of us to lie down," I snapped back at him.

By the time I turned again to the Erdian frying pan, a hatch had opened, and three Erdian guards were marching down the handle. They looked just like Amp. They wore helmets and held tiny zapper guns like the one Amp had brought with him when he arrived on Earth. The weapons looked like TV remote controls. These zappers didn't do anything more than give you a little shock of static electricity, but I didn't think this was the time to bring that up.

The guards split up and scrambled about the boat, using blue laser beams to search all its corners, including our bodies. They flipped and tumbled about like crazed Smurfs who had had way too much coffee. We watched their circus act in silence.

Amp didn't move.

I figured they were searching us and the boat for weapons or threatening behavior. Once finished and satisfied we weren't dangerous, a guard whispered something into his wristband.

Then one guard stood watching me, and

another stood in front of Olivia and eyed her with suspicion. I figured the third Erdian guard was behind me, watching Mr. Larry like a hawk.

"Hey, you look like Amp's ugly twin brother," I said to my guard.

He flinched and tilted his head to the side. He clearly didn't speak English. He raised his zapper and squinted at me.

"Maybe we should see if you can swim, small fry," I said, which only made him look more puzzled.

"Please don't talk to the royal guards," Amp begged me. "You'll make a mess of this."

"Isn't it pretty impossible to make this situation any messier? My planet is being attacked by blue space aliens!"

A short and plump Erdian emerged from the hatch and proceeded down the handle of the frying pan. At first I thought this was the Kaloofa, but when this Erdian started throwing what looked like baby powder everywhere, I knew it must be a strange Erdian ceremony.

Before long, the handle of the ship and much of the boat was covered in the white dust. I decided to just go with the flow.

Then the powder thrower Erdian lay down like Amp.

After waiting in awkward silence for thirty seconds, a very ordinary-looking Erdian emerged. She looked just like Amp, too, except she wore bulky boots made of white, fluffy fur. She stood up very straight and held her chin high. Instead of a helmet, she wore a wreath of what looked like dried seaweed on her head.

My first Kaloofa.

Amp once told me Erdians weren't boys or girls, but it was almost impossible for Olivia and I not to think of Erdians as either boys or girls. It was probably a habit from dealing with humans our whole lives. Perhaps because Kaloofa ended in an *a*, I thought of her as a girl. Or maybe it was the ridiculous boots. No matter what I did, I was sure Amp would say I was already making a mess of it.

At that moment the Kaloofa looked my way. I held up two fingers in a peace sign. "Greetings, your worship."

She looked at me like I had just burped, and she turned away snootily. Oops. Strike one with the ol' Kaloofa.

She walked up to Amp, who was still on his back like a stiff, dead weasel.

That was when an idea hit me: This doesn't have to turn into a war! This was our chance to prevent a war. The Erdians needed to know they were picking on the wrong planet.

After all, the Erdians hadn't started firing yet. There must be a reason for that. They had totally blown the element of surprise, which must be a big deal. And I was sure all the soldiers had seen this cloud of spaceships drop out of the sky and settle over the lake. They were probably spreading the news right now.

The chances were slim, but fighting was not our only option here.

And I had Olivia; she could talk her way out of anything. Just ask my school's principal, Mr. Luntz; Olivia had talked us out of a dozen of his detentions. Maybe she could do the same with an interplanetary war.

The next few minutes would determine the future of my planet and all the humans on it.

We better not mess this up.

10

Talking Tough

The Kaloofa and Amp exchanged words for a minute—at least I thought it was words. I couldn't understand any of it. They were talking Erdian. It sounded like static on the radio with bird chirps and guinea pig grunts mixed in.

Finally she waved her three-fingered hand, and Amp hopped up and began speaking even more rapidly in Erdian, pointing at Olivia and me. I caught two Erdian words I knew: *floofy* and *brimples*. The rest of it was a complete mystery.

The Kaloofa didn't look impressed. She even crossed her arms and tapped one of her hairy boots, the intergalactic symbol of *You're boring me to death*.

Poor Amp. The more he explained and the more excited he got, the worse it looked for us.

His body language told me he needed help.

It was time to get tough.

"Hey, can I say something?" I interrupted.

They both looked at me like I had farted. Strike two for Zack McGee.

Boy, these Erdians were snooty.

"Does she speak English, like you?" I asked.

Amp shook his head. "No. She never bothered. It takes several weeks of training to learn your language, which is sort of below an Erdian royal."

"Several weeks?" I said. "Gosh, I'm still trying to figure it out after ten years."

"It's a relatively simple language compared to many," he said. "I'm sure the Kaloofa didn't think it was worth the trouble."

I growled. "Let's not even get into how rude that is."

"Yes, let's not," he said, shooting a nervous, sideways glance at the Kaloofa.

"Well, then, can you translate something for me? Why don't you tell your queen this: You're messing with the wrong planet, missy. We humans are ready to whup some Erdian butt. We'll knock the snot out of your antennas. You want to dance? Oh, we are so ready to dance, sister. So why don't you take your seaweed hat and go back through that wormhole in space and time you crawled out of."

Amp stared at me with his mouth hanging open.

"You tell 'em, Zack," Olivia's grandfather said from behind me.

"Go ahead," I said, snapping my fingers. "Tell her that."

"Excuse me—I have a better idea," Olivia said, raising her hand.

"Oh, thank goodness," Amp said.

Olivia looked up and appeared to be composing her message. "Amp, why don't you tell Mrs. Kaloofa that we welcome her to Earth. We are glad and humbled to meet someone of her stature."

"What's a stature?" I asked.

Amp nodded and proceeded to translate what Olivia said.

The Kaloofa made a small bow toward Olivia.

"Hey, what about the stuff I said?" I grumbled.

Olivia ignored me. "Now tell her we are your friends. We helped and protected you when your ship crashed and you were injured."

"But I wasn't injured," Amp said.

"I know, but just tell her that," Olivia said. "It sounds better. Tell her we fed you like a little baby bird who fell out of a nest."

"Wait! What nest?" Amp asked, puzzled.

"Yeah, say we fed you with one of those little bird feeders," I said.

"Wait! What the heck is a bird feeder?" Amp shouted.

Olivia laughed. "It's a little dropper thingy. It doesn't really matter. Just tell her that Zack and I nursed you back to health because we are kind and caring. Doesn't matter if it's true or not—it sounds great. Go ahead. Translate that."

He did, and the Kaloofa looked very interested in the story. She looked at me and Olivia once more, like she hadn't noticed us the first time.

We were getting somewhere. I decided that Olivia's plan might work better than my get-tough approach.

"And now tell her that we are only children. But we kept you a secret from the grown-ups. We hid you from the adults who would treat you like a virus. For months we protected you and made you healthy again."

"He even lived in my room," I said, snapping at Olivia. "Tell her that. He's, like, the galaxy's most annoying roommate. Think of the sacrifices I made. I almost flunked out of fourth grade!"

"Hey, you are not exactly a well-mannered scholar," Amp said defensively.

"And we even tried to fix his *Dingle*," I said to Olivia.

"Oh dear, what is a *Dingle* and how did he break it?" Olivia's grandfather asked. "Sounds painful."

"It's just the terrible name he gave his space-ship," I answered.

"The *Dingle* has saved you more than once, young man!" Amp shouted, pointing at me.

"Yes, Zack, that's so good!" Olivia agreed. She looked at Amp. "We even tried to help you repair your broken ship and launch it. We did that for you. Say all that."

Amp hesitated but then translated, pointing to

Olivia and me several times.

I could tell all this was making an impression on the Kaloofa.

When he was finished, Amp looked at Olivia. "Anything else?"

Olivia chewed on her lip. "I'm thinking."

"Will they still attack, Amp?" I asked.

"I'm not so sure they will," he said. "But it's an Erdian custom to make a peace offering in a situation like this. Something grand. Something impressive."

"How about a nifty little rowboat?" I asked.

"This junky, leaky, stolen vehicle? You're can't be serious!" Amp exclaimed.

"Or what about our truck?" Olivia suggested. "It runs great."

"You mean *my* truck?" Olivia's grandfather protested from behind me. "I just put in a new transmission."

Amp stomped his foot. "C'mon, guys! That squeaky, old truck and this leaky boat are not what I had in mind. Quick! We need to offer something they can't get anywhere else in the universe. Something befitting Erdian royalty. Something you can only get here on Earth."

We floated in silence, thinking.

My stomach growled loudly, and everyone looked at me.

That was when I got the best idea in human history.

"I've got it," I said finally. "It's perfect. A peace offering every Erdian would love."

"What is it?" Olivia asked.

I smiled. "We'll just need a little help from those National Guard soldiers."

11

Peace Offering

Moving a great idea from your brain into the real world is sometimes harder than you ever imagined.

And to put my idea into action, I needed to get back to the dock and all those National Guard soldiers. I'd have to sell them on my plan for a suitable peace offering to the Erdians and get the soldiers help in pulling it off. Then I'd save the world.

Easier said than done.

My plan hit a roadblock before it even got underway.

"Uh . . . . we need to get back to the dock," I announced, once the Kaloofa and her guards had returned to her spaceship and left our powder-covered rowboat floating in the still lake water.

"Afraid the battery is all used up," Olivia's grandfather said.

"Which way is the dock?" Olivia asked. "All I can see are trees."

Amp looked around. "There are no flattened implements with which to propel this vessel," Amp said.

"Can you speak English, please?" I mumbled.

Olivia sighed. "He means there are no oars to paddle this rowboat."

"Oh," I said. "We already knew that."

So we sat in silence, thinking. My stomach growled again.

"We could scream for help," Olivia suggested. "Maybe the soldiers will come out and rescue us."

"Not sure they'd hear us," Amp said.

"And besides," I said, pointing up, "nobody wants to come out here with a cloud of alien ships hanging over their heads."

Everyone looked up at the spaceships. They had risen in unison to about one hundred feet above the lake's surface. It was as if they were all staring at me, waiting to see my great plan take shape. I would have started sweating, but my flesh had been chilled numb.

"C'mon, guys," I said, throwing up my arms. "The world is counting on us."

"No pressure, right?" Olivia said, shooting me a look.

"Who is the best swimmer here?" Amp asked.

"Forget it," Olivia said. "Water's too cold. You'd drown."

"Oh, I didn't mean me," Amp replied quietly.

I picked up an old soda bottle that was lying on the bottom of the boat. "Does anyone have a piece of paper and a pen?" I asked. Mr. Larry fished around in his vest pockets and pulled out a crumpled Chinese food menu and a black Sharpie. "That'll do," I said.

"Are you writing your last will and testament?" Amp asked. "I believe that's what humans do in such situations."

"No," I said slowly. "I'm saving us. I'm going to put a note in this bottle and throw it to the shore."

"Zack, even you can't throw it that far," Olivia cut in. "If we're going to do it, we need a way to launch it, like we did the first time with Amp."

"Oh, and that worked so well," Amp said, lip-farting. Until now, I had no idea he could even make that sound.

"Well," Mr. Larry said. "I have a hose and some duct tape." He pulled both from his vest. "And it looks like someone left an old paper towel tube behind."

"What good does any of that do us?" I said, remembering how we needed water and a bike pump and a hundred other things we didn't have to launch Amp the first time.

"Think backward," Mr. Larry said. "We can use the air in the bottle to propel the rocket. We just have to cut a piece of the paper tube off," he said, doing it as he explained. "And then wrap the note around it."

It was so crazy I thought it just might work. We even found an old Ping-Pong ball and used that as a cap for the rocket by taping it on with, like, ten feet of duct tape. We connected the paper-tube rocket (with the note) to the hose, which we taped tightly to the bottle. Amp used his alien know-how to aim it toward the shore. And when it was all ready, I got the honor of stomping on the bottle since it was my idea. And I am the best stomper.

Olivia counted down, "3, 2, 1 . . ." And the note took off up into the night sky, disappearing for a moment against the moon, and then arcing back down twenty feet from the boat with a barely audible *sploosh*.

We sat in that boat for five long minutes after. The only sound came from my unhappy stomach.

Once it became clear none of my fellow passengers had any other ideas, one popped into my head.

"Hey, Amp, can your ship retrace its steps?" I asked.

"Steps? It doesn't have feet," Amp said, pointing to his ship as if to prove his point.

Olivia growled. "He means, does it remember where the dock is?" Olivia said. "You know, can it return to the spot it picked Zack up?"

"Picked me up?" I croaked. "You mean punched me out."

Amp tapped his foot and considered the question. "Why, yes, I guess it can do that rather easily. See, my ship is equipped with global positioning technology that—"

"I don't care how it works," I interrupted, "just that it does work."

"Of course you don't," Amp said with a huff. "Well, you've ridden on this ship enough times in one night. I guess one more ride won't kill you."

"No way," I said. "I'm not riding on that thing again. I think I'm too cold and stiff to hold on for another flight."

"Okay, then," Amp said, turning to Olivia, "once I get in there, you hold on to my ship tightly."

"No, she is not doing that, either," I said.

Amp became annoyed. "Well, I'm afraid Mr. Larry is much too heavy for my ship's damaged stabilizers to support. We'd sink like a very large stone." Amp seemed to consider what he had said and then looked over my shoulder at Olivia's grandfather. "No offense. I didn't mean to call you heavy, it's just that—"

"No offense taken," Olivia grandfather said.

"We need all of us to get back," I said. "Olivia, give me your one of your shoelaces."

"What are you thinking?" she asked.

I watched as she unlaced one of her shoes. "A boat like this is built smooth on the bottom, right? There's very little resistance, so it doesn't take too much energy to move it across the water."

"You're going to row this boat with a shoe-lace?" Amp asked, shaking his head in confusion.

I laughed as I took Olivia's shoelace and pushed past her. Olivia and I switched seats, and the boat rocked in the water. I started to tie the lace to the hook at front of the boat.

"He's going to have that spaceship tow us

back," Olivia's grandfather said.

"Oh, clever," Amp said, nodding. "This could actually work."

"Good thinking, Zack," Olivia said. "Miss Martin would be proud of you."

I rolled my eyes at the thought of our teacher at Reed Elementary School. Sometimes she seemed shocked when I could remember where my desk was. I had come a long way since Amp had arrived.

"Zack, when you mentioned how this boat is smooth on the bottom and has little resistance to the water, you're actually talking about drag."

"Oh no, it's another—"

Amp began speaking into his annoying wrist recorder:

"Note to Erdian Council . . ."

"Please, not now, Amp," Olivia begged.
But once Amp started, he couldn't help himself.

"Earth children are aware of the mechanical force of drag, they just don't know the name of it. Of course, drag is the force generated when a solid object moves through liquid or air, as in the case of a boat or a plane. Of course, when I travel through space, my ship does not get slowed down by drag because there is no air in space. No resistance, no drag."

"Are you almost done?" I interrupted.
He continued:

"Essentially, drag acts in the opposite direction of a moving

object's motion and can be thought of as friction between the object's surface and the fluid it's moving through. That's why Zack instinctively knows a boat's bottom is smooth to reduce drag so the boat moves easier across the surface of the water. An interesting subject but, apparently, we don't have time for more. Scout Amp, over and out."

I let out a big breath. "Okay, back to business. Getting to that dock is just step one, guys. The hard part of this plan is still ahead of us."

"Even the longest journey begins with the first step," Olivia's grandfather said.

We all thought about that for moment.

"Step one, coming up," Amp said, and climbed into the *Dingle*.

12

Shopping Spree

Amp had once told me that the Erdians believed there was always a way to accomplish something, no matter how difficult it seemed at first.

I guess I had taken that lesson to heart.

Because as I stood in front of the angry crowd of soldiers, scientists, and mysterious government agents, I had my doubts.

"You want us to give the aliens what?" barked a gray-haired man in a fancy general's uniform.

I gulped and felt myself shrink a little bit.

We were surrounded. There was nowhere left to run or hide. The three of us were backed up to the end of the dock, right where we had climbed out of the rowboat. Amp's ship was now parked at my feet, but he had not emerged.

I gulped. "Ritz Crackers, sir," I repeated. "We'll need every box we can find in town."

"You mean the little round crackers?" said Mr. Prentiss, who had pushed his way to the front of crowd. "But why Ritz Crackers? Why not graham crackers? Or those little soup crackers? This makes no sense."

"I think this kid has gone crackers himself, sir," said Sarge to the general. Sarge still looked like he wanted to throw me into the lake. I gave him a little wave. He did not return the gesture.

"I can only tell you what I know will work," I said.

Mr. Prentiss smiled at me. "General, I know this boy," he said, turning to him. "He's clever. Has a good mind for science. And so does his friend Olivia. I think we should trust these kids. Nobody knows these aliens better than they do."

I stood up as tall as I could. "Yes, and that's why we need Ritz Crackers. A whole lot of them."

"Let me get this straight," the general thundered. "You want us to go on a shopping spree? For Ritz Crackers? And these invaders will leave us alone? Preposterous!"

91

"That's correct," Olivia said, stepping up next to me. "Your men will have to go into town and buy as many as they can. Load up your trucks. The faster, the better. Superpronto."

"Superpronto?" the general repeated with a sour, disgusted face. "I'll look like a fool." He glanced up at the thousands of Erdian spacecrafts that waited over the lake.

"Trust me," I said. "Erdians love Ritz Crackers. It's the perfect peace offering. I doubt they make them anywhere else in the universe." I cleared my throat nervously. "And . . . as long as you're getting the crackers, we should sweeten the deal with SweeTarts. Buy as many as you—"

"WHAT?!" the general roared. "Should I start making a shopping list?" He was so angry, the crowd seemed to inch away from him.

"Oh, and pick up sunflower seeds, too," Olivia said. "Tons of those. Add that to the list. Amp likes to eat those for dessert."

"Sunflower . . . ," the general began, but could not finish.

I held up a finger. "Oh, make sure they're the already-shelled kind. Amp doesn't like cracking off those salty shells."

"No salty shells," the general repeated, as if he couldn't believe what he was hearing.

Mr. Prentiss kneeled in front of us. "Zack, Olivia," he said soothingly, "are you saying that if we give the aliens as many Ritz Crackers, Swee-Tarts, and sunflower seeds as we can buy, we'll prevent the aliens from attacking?"

"Exactly," I said. "At least, that's what I think will happen."

"You're not sure!" boomed the general.

"It's a pretty good idea," Olivia said, putting a hand on my shoulder. "This could work." She knelt on the dock's rough boards and knocked on the side of Amp's spaceship. "Get out here right now, you big chicken," she said loudly.

Everyone stared at the *Dingle*. After several moments the hatch popped open, and Amp stuck his head out. "Good evening, everyone. Oh, wait, I'm sorry. Should I be saying good morning? How embarrassing."

The crowd—even Mr. Prentiss—gasped and jumped back three feet. Amp squinted as several flashlights from the soldiers lit him up. He held a hand up to block the light.

"Whoa! Easy on the eyes!" he shouted. "Listen to Zack and Olivia," he said. "Their idea is better than any I can come up with. And, to be honest, I can't get enough of those crackers and candies. The Kaloofa will love them."

"Kaloofa?" Sarge growled.

"Am I . . . Am I just supposed to put all this on my credit c-card?" the general stammered. "I'll have to get the proper approvals. Wake my superiors. Run this up the chain of command."

"There's no time for that," Olivia said. "It's unclear how long they're going to wait before they start vaporizing people."

"Nice," I whispered to Olivia.

This seemed to settle the issue.

"We'll put it all on mine," Mr. Prentiss said, pulling a credit card out of his wallet. "I'll bill you later, General. Now . . . I'll need volunteers to take me into town with several of your large trucks."

"I'll volunteer," Sarge said. "This is just too good and too weird to miss."

As much of the crowd headed back down the dock to go on their junk-food shopping spree, my parents came pushing though in the other direction. They were crying. They hugged me. They hugged Olivia. They even hugged Olivia's grandfather.

But the moment they laid eyes on Amp watching from the hatch of his spaceship, they froze.

"Mom and Dad, I'd like to introduce you to Amp," I said. "He's been living at our house for the last couple of months."

You should have seen their faces.

13

Breakfast Meeting

I paced around the end of the dock, surrounded by a wall of at least four hundred boxes of Ritz Crackers, SweeTarts, and sunflower seeds.

I was nervously popping fistfuls of SweeTarts into my mouth and crunching them to dust. Of course, I was twitching with nerves and excitement, but I also was so hungry, I would have gladly eaten several of the cardboard boxes, too.

"You sure all this food wasn't just for you, kid?" Sarge asked me.

I didn't answer.

Luckily, one of the soldiers interrupted. He produced some blankets, and I was now wrapped like an upright burrito.

"Why aren't they coming to get their food?" the general asked for the fourth time.

"I don't know," I said, making big eyes at Amp.

"Me? I don't know, either," Amp said, shrugging his tiny blue shoulders. "I can't reach anybody with my communication system."

"Not too many sweets," Mom said. "You had three cavities filled this year alone."

"Sweet tooth," Mr. Prentiss said to me with a wink.

My parents hadn't been able to stop staring with slightly disgusted looks on their faces at Amp,

like they had discovered a blue rat had been hiding in the walls of their home.

The Erdian spaceships remained stubbornly fixed in the air above the lake, as they had all night long. The sky was now turning a dark purple, which indicated the sun would soon be joining the party.

Without warning, Olivia suddenly hopped off one of the boxes and looked around. "I know what we should do!"

The crowd of soldiers, scientists, secret agents, and my parents turned to Olivia.

She sighed. "Look at all of you. This dock is more crowded than an elevator. Think about it. A crowd this size is a security risk. The Kaloofa might trust Zack and me, but she doesn't know all of you from Adam."

"Wait, who's Adam?" I whispered.

She shook off my question. "Now, all of you, beat it. Get off this dock."

"Young lady," the general started in, "I am not accustomed to being spoken to in such a—"

"Especially you, General," Olivia interrupted. "You're even scaring me, and I'm from this planet." She started shooing the crowd down the dock with her hands. "C'mon, all you, go watch from the beach. You're giving the Erdian empress the creeps."

Unbelievably, the adults listened to her. In less than a minute the dock was cleared of onlookers. Just Olivia, Amp, and I remained.

We peered up at the cloud and spaceships and, just like Olivia had predicted, the Kaloofa's frying pan ship soon emerged and descended slowly down to the dock, the handle of her ship eventually settling at the very end.

The whole process started again. Three guards emerged first and searched the dock with their

blue beams of light. Soon they were standing at attention, but I couldn't tell if the puny guard who watched me was the same one from earlier. Next the same powder thrower emerged and blanketed the dock with clouds of baby powder. Then the powder thrower lay down, facing up in the same stiff pose as earlier on the boat. I glanced over at Amp, and he was doing the same thing.

Erdians were so weird.

The Kaloofa and her boots soon joined us. Olivia and I grabbed some samples of our peace offering and watched as the Kaloofa examined the goods we placed before her in the palms of our hands.

She took a cracker and cautiously nibbled at it, then promptly proceeded to quickly devour a dozen of the crackers, spinning each in circles and gnawing at them like a crazed termite. Soon a pile of cracker dust surrounded her boots. The Swee-Tarts were next, which she fed into her mouth and crunched with shocking speed and enthusiasm.

When Olivia and I smiled at the sight of the great Erdian empress wolfing down candy like there was no tomorrow, she stopped mid-chew and considered us. After a moment she snatched up some sunflower seeds and popped them into her mouth and smacked her lips in delight.

"Whoa, you must have been starving, Kaloof," Olivia said with a giggle.

Amp flinched. "Please don't call her Kaloof. That is terribly rude."

"How was that for a yummy peace offering, eh?" I asked the empress.

Clearly, she didn't understand us. But she looked satisfied and pleased for sure.

And she turned and walked back up the handle of her ship. The guards and powder thrower quickly followed.

Olivia and I looked at each other. We high-fived.

After a few tense moments the spaceships began lining up next to the dock. Thousands of them. The crowd on the beach clapped and cheered. Amp was jumping up and down. Olivia and I hugged each other with a combination of pride and excitement.

For the next two hours we distributed our peace offering to what must have been twenty thousand tiny spaceships. It was tiring but exhilarating, as well.

The idea that Olivia and I had just saved the world from destruction was thrilling enough to fuel both of us for several weeks.

We had done it.

"We saved the world," I kept repeating over and over.

14

Hero's Good-Bye

I could get used to this hero thing.

A cheerful, festive celebration was underway on the beach. The sun was lifting above the trees, and the air had warmed nicely.

One of the soldiers had produced a small speaker, and he had plugged it into his cell phone. Dance music with a fast-thumping beat swept over the sand.

I was perched up high up on my dad's shoulders as he spun and danced around. Olivia was on her grandfather's shoulders. We were receiving high fives from the soldiers, who happily snacked on whatever Ritz Crackers and SweeTarts the Erdians had been unable to fit into their ships.

Even the general had pulled off his shoes and now danced barefoot in the sand with a laughing

female soldier. He kept looking my way and giving me thumbs-ups.

Mom was weeping happy tears as she used her phone to snap photos and video of the jubilation. I couldn't wait to show them to my little brother later so he could see what he'd missed. Even my aunt Joni might finally be impressed with what her flakey nephew had done.

Mr. Prentiss was waving his credit card around, entertaining two soldiers with stories of shocked grocery store clerks who had never sold so much to a single customer.

It was quite the scene.

I was only in the fourth grade, but it occurred to me that this morning might just be the best moment of my life. Certainly top five, even if I lived to be one hundred.

How can you beat saving the world?

That was when, from the corner of my eye, I noticed one last spaceship hovering alongside the dock. One remaining Erdian was standing there, watching us. It was Amp.

I knew what was happening by the way he stood; his shoulders were slumped, his chin had dropped to his chest, and his six blue fingers clutched nervously at his belly.

Amp was leaving.

Leaving me.

Leaving Olivia.

Leaving us.

Leaving Earth.

"AMP!" I shouted. I scrambled down from my dad's shoulders.

Olivia looked back over her shoulder at the sound of alarm in my voice.

"OLIVIA, LOOK!" I shouted.

Her face fell.

Soon we were racing over the sand as fast as we could. We pounded down the boards of the dock. My breath seemed to get stuck in my clenched throat.

I could feel the crowd stopping to watch us from the beach, somehow understanding that they should keep their distance.

Nobody liked to share in good-byes.

"You don't have to—" I began.

He held up both hands, cutting me off. "The time has come, my friend." He pointed to the sky, where the entire fleet of Erdian spaceships hovered silently high up. "They're all waiting for me."

Olivia fell to her knees. "Now? How about staying a few more weeks? In the summer we'll have a lot more time to—"

His shaking head stopped her. "Sorry. It sounds great. But it has come time for me to go back. I've learned so much from you both. I've grown so fond of you two odd creatures. But on this planet I am a stranger in a strange land."

I knelt down and put my face in front of him. I sniffed. My eyes were filling with hot tears, despite my best effort to keep that from happening. "Stay for the party, at least. Say good-bye to everyone," I said in a strained, croaky voice.

He let out a deep sigh. "I don't know them," he said with a crooked smile. "I really know only you two. You are the ones I will take with me in my three hearts."

"You have three

hearts?" Olivia whispered, tears starting to roll down her face. "See, we didn't even know that."

"It just never came up," Amp said with a shrug. "Now, look, I've made your eyes start to sweat."

Olivia laughed through her tears. "This isn't sweat, Amp."

I wiped my face with the back of my hand. "Hey, you can stay in touch, right? Come back and visit? Write letters? Send us messages?"

He smiled and shook his head. "You know that's impossible, Zack. It's too far, too risky. You both know this is my best opportunity to get back to where I belong."

"But your ship is broken," Olivia said. "You can't fly."

"Oh, it's been repaired," he said, glancing back at the *Dingle*. "Erdians always bring plenty of spare parts when so many travel through space and time."

"Oh, shoot," Olivia said, pushing her face up next to mine. "What are we going to do with ourselves without you to babysit?"

"You're going to have happy, normal lives. I am so proud to know both of you. You have extended so much kindness to me. I will never forget you."

"Well, I guess this is really is good-bye then," I said, smiling through my tears.

"I wish I could cry like you two," Amp said. "It must feel so interesting. He lifted his wrist to his mouth and announced:

"Note to Erdian Council . . ."

"No!" I said.

"Just joking," he said, dropping his arm. "Got you." He sighed. "Now let me hug your faces."

He reached up on his tippy toes and hugged my face, then Olivia's.

"Gross, you both got me all wet!" he said, pretending to be annoyed.

We were both too broken up to even smile at his attempt at humor.

"You two will do great things," he said in a clipped voice. With that, he spun around and, with two quick hops, disappeared into his ship, the tiny hatch closing behind him.

After a few seconds the *Dingle* shot off like a silent rocket.

It was so odd to see his spaceship work the way it was supposed to. We watched it rise, like when you let go of a helium balloon and follow its flight path for as long as you can. Soon we lost track of it as it joined the thousands of other ships high up in the sky.

A moment later the entire swarm of Erdian ships, stuffed with Ritz Crackers, SweeTarts, and sunflower seeds, shot off in neat rows. The sky flashed when the ships exited our atmosphere.

In just seconds they were all gone.

And so was Amp.

Olivia and I hugged for a full minute.

"We'll never forget him," Olivia said. "At least we'll always have that."

As we headed back down the dock to the crowd of onlookers, I knew she was right. We would be in Amp's three hearts, and I would have my memory of him in mine—no matter how much space and time separated us.

He hadn't even been here that long, but I was a different kind of a kid for knowing him.

I was such a mess when he arrived.

Now anything seemed possible. I believed I

could do whatever I set my mind to. I might just do great things after all, like Amp had said.

Like two balls that collide on a pool table, I'd been knocked in a different direction when Amp had come crashing into my life.

And for that I would always be grateful.

THE END

Try It Yourself: Stomp Rocket

When Olivia, Zack, Amp, and Mr. Larry are stuck in the middle of the lake with a dead battery and an emergency on their hands, they hatch a plan to use pieces of trash from the bottom of the boat to launch a message to the shore, using a rocket.

In this experiment, you'll use recycled materials to build a "stomp rocket" that can reach heights up to a hundred feet in the air!

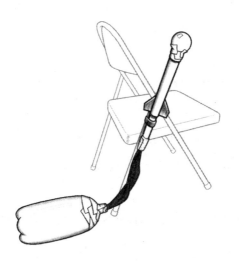

For this project, you'll need:

- A two-liter bottle or milk jug
- A piece of flexible hose that can fit or stretch over the jug's mouth. An old bicycle inner tube works well.
- A sheet of paper
- Cardboard for fins
- Scissors
- Duct tape
- A Ping-Pong ball
- 14–20 inches of any rigid, smooth pipe or tube—like a ¾ inch PVC pipe
- Something you can tape the launcher tube to, like a folding chair or bookend
- An adult to help with safety—but not to do the project for you!

Stage 1: Build the Launcher

1. Cut the bicycle inner tube or flexible hose to about 18 inches long. A bit shorter or longer is fine.
2. Insert one end of the rigid pipe about one

inch into the inner tube.

3. Fold the slack of the inner tube tight around the pipe, and duct tape it in place with a few wraps.

4. Insert the mouth of the two-liter bottle into the other end of the inner tube and tape the tube securely onto the bottle.

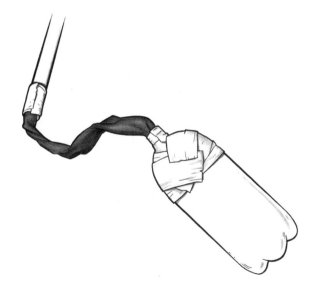

5. Tape the rigid tube to the stand you found (like a folding chair or bookend) so it aims nearly straight up. Make sure at least 12 inches of the tube is sticking freely above the stand. You'll need this to make and launch the rocket.

Stage 2: Make the Rocket

1. Wrap the paper around the launch tube and tape it so it's *almost* a tight fit but can still smoothly slide up and down. You may need to cinch the paper tighter by grabbing the inside corner and coiling the paper inward.

2. Stack the protruding wraps flat and tape the tube near the top and bottom. This is the rocket's fuselage.

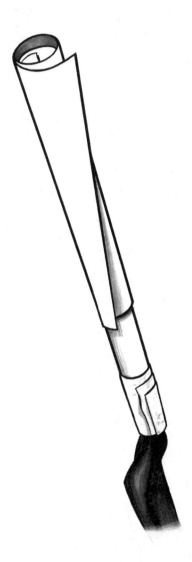

3. Keeping the fuselage on the launch tube to support the paper from the inside, place the Ping-Pong ball on top of the tube and use several shorter pieces of tape to attach it to the top of the rocket. Add enough tape that no air can sneak between the fuselage and the Ping-Pong ball.

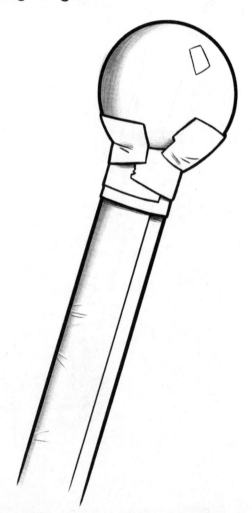

4. Use the scissors to cut your favorite shape of rocket fins and tape them on the bottom of the fuselage.

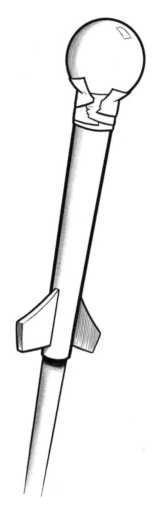

5. Decorate the rocket if you wish!

Stage 3: Launch Test

1. Clear the area! Make sure the people around you know you're going to launch a rocket. Remember what rockets do after they go up: They come back down. Everybody nearby should be thinking about this.

2. Make sure the launch tube is secure and that it's pointing almost straight up.

3. Ensure the rocket slides smoothly up and down on the launch tube, and then leave it on the tube, ready for launch.

4. Safety Tip 1: Make sure the rocket will go up in the air only—never toward anybody!

5. Safety Tip 2: With every experiment, it's safest to "start small" so you can learn how a new system works before you increase the energy level.

6. Yell out a countdown, and *step* (don't stomp) onto the bottle. How did it work?

Stage 4: Big Launch!

1. To reset, blow high-pressure air from your lungs back into the bottle through the launch tube. The pressure should reinflate it. You can also squeeze the bottle back open with your hands to help.

2. Slide the rocket back onto the launch tube.

3. Now it's time to go big! Yell out a loud countdown and give the bottle a great big stomp!

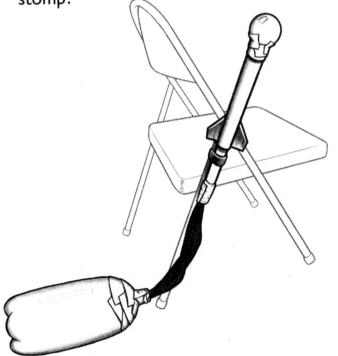

Experiments

Now that you've got a reliable launch system, you can start doing some experiments to discover how to make your rocket go higher! Here are a few things you may want to learn more about:

Discover:

Which parts of the system are the most important in making the rocket go high? Try changing something about the setup:

- Make a shorter or longer rocket
- Try taping a smaller or bigger bottle to the end of the hose
- Change the length of the hose

Which changes make the biggest difference in launch height? Remember to only change one thing at a time! Otherwise you won't know which change made the difference.

Test:

What launch angle makes a rocket go the farthest?
Make sure *nobody* is downrange during this test!

- Start with a high angle, launch the rocket, and mark where it landed.
- Progressively lower the launch angle, marking where each launch hits the ground. Try taking a photograph of each launch angle, and hold up fingers in the photo for which launch it is so you can figure out which angle went the farthest.

Improvise:

What ideas does this project give you? What would it take to test them out? Run your ideas by an adult, and then get out there and try them yourself! It's a big and wonderful world out there, and the more you try, the more you'll learn. And the more you learn, the more you can do!

Blast from the Past

Turn the page for the experiment from the first Alien in My Pocket book.

Try it again now and see if the outcome is any different.

Try It Yourself:
Bottle Rocket Blastoff

Rockets work by pushing exhaust downward (really fast), which pushes the rocket upward (really fast). You can build your own bottle rocket that uses air pressure to push water downward out of the rocket, which will propel the rocket upward for a big launch.

YOU WILL NEED: 2-liter soda bottle, cardboard, duct tape, a bicycle pump with a pressure gauge, an inflation needle, a rubber stopper, and some stakes.

Building Your Rocket

1. Make sure the rubber stopper can be inserted into the end of the soda bottle so it holds air inside. You can check for a seal by squeezing the bottle when the stopper is pushed

2. With the help of an adult, drill a small hole through the stopper so that when you push the inflation needle in, it fits tightly. Try starting with a smaller drill bit than you think you'll need, and redrill the hole bigger later if you really need to. The goal is to have the rubber tight around the needle, making a good seal.

3. Push the inflation needle through the rubber stopper till the end pokes out a little bit. The end with the small hole should be poking out of the smaller tapered end of the stopper.

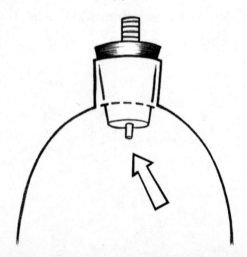

4. Add fins and a nose cone to your bottle to turn it into a rocket! You can design them however you want. Putting the fins near the rocket's nozzle will help it go straight.

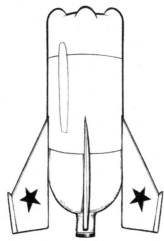

5. Build a launchpad by driving some stakes or sticks into the ground so that your rocket can sit upright while you're pumping the air in.

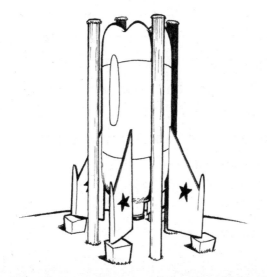

3

6. Attach the bike pump's nozzle to the inflation needle that's now going through the stopper. Now we're ready to fly!

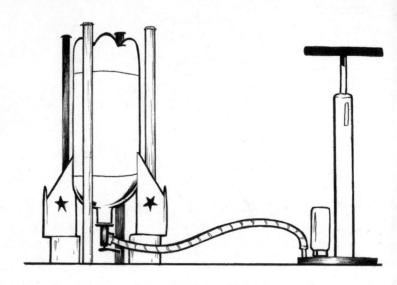

Launch Sequence

1. When you don't know how something works yet, it's always safer to start small. Do an air test by gently pushing the stopper into the nozzle. Put the rocket on the launchpad and pump air into the bottle till the stopper pops out. Try to watch the pressure gauge on the bike pump and see what pressure made the stopper pop out.

2. Do a second air test by pushing the stopper into the rocket nozzle with a little bit more force than last time. Put the rocket back on the pad and pump again till the stopper pops out. You may see a little launch this time, and it should have taken more pressure than last time to force the stopper out. Cool! All systems are "go" for launch.

3. Put some water in the bottle, push the stopper back in, stand back, and start pumping! This time, the rocket should get at least a little launch if the pressure was around 10 PSI or higher before the stopper popped out. Now your rocket works; it's time to do some experiments!

Experiment Time

1. Try varying the amount of force you use to insert the stopper each time. What happens when you push it in very lightly versus with more force? How does it change the pressure required for a launch?

2. Change the amount of water you put in the rocket for each launch. What other important property of the rocket changes when you add lots of water versus a little bit?

5

3. Test out some different nose cones. Does the rocket fly better with a big, long nose cone that's heavy? How about a short one that uses less material?
4. Vary the size and placement of the fins. What would you need to do to make the rocket spin on its way up?

Tips

- When you're trying to learn about something by changing things, it's important to only change one thing at a time so you can see what a difference it made. That means if you're trying out different nose cones, try to use the same amount of water and air pressure for each launch. That way, if the rocket's flight changes from trial to trial, you know it's because of the different nose cone and not something else.
- If you think you have an idea that explains how something works, think of ways to test out if that idea is true! Do you think that the air pressure is related to how high the rocket flies? How would you test that out?
- Be patient with yourself! When you're trying something new, it might not work right the first or second or third time you try it. Maybe even more times than

that. Learn by making observations about the rocket's performance so you can make the right adjustments as you proceed.

Safety Notes

- Rockets store and release a lot of energy! Always make sure that if the rocket were to launch when you don't expect it to, it won't hit anything or anybody that's nearby.
- Make sure everybody around knows that you're going to launch when you're pumping air into the rocket. Doing a countdown helps, especially if you know how many pumps it takes to launch your rocket.
- If you've pumped a lot of air into the rocket and the pressure is high but the rocket's not launching, don't go up to the rocket and try to pull the stopper out. It might launch before you're ready and hit you! Instead, wait till the pressure dies down and reinsert the stopper with less force than you used last time.

Dedication and Thanks

This series is dedicated to my parents, John and Sarah, whose bold support of my childhood interests catalyzed a lifetime of joyful experimentation and learning.

Bringing big new ideas from imagination to reality is rarely the work of a single person, and Alien in My Pocket is no exception. Sincere appreciation and thanks are due to many people—especially my creative and collaborative editor, Dave Linker; my fabulous agent, Linda Loewenthal; the amazing Macky Pamintuan, whose art exceeds my own imagination; and the incredibly talented Dave Keane for breathing life and laughter into these characters and their adventures.

Onward, upward—for science!

Nate Ball

ALIEN IN MY POCKET

Read all the Alien in My Pocket books today!

Visit **www.alieninmypocket.com**
for science facts, experiments, and more!

HARPER
An Imprint of HarperCollinsPublishers

www.harpercollinschildrens.com